I'll Always Love You

By HANS WILHELM

Picture Knight

HODDER AND STOUGHTON

To Lea

British Library Cataloguing in Publication Data

Wilhelm, Hans
  I'll always love you.
  I. Title
  813'.54[J]   PZ7
   ISBN 0-340-40153-2

Text and illustrations copyright © Hans Wilhelm, Inc. 1985

First published 1985 by Crown Publishers, Inc., New York, USA
First published in Great Britain 1985 by Hodder and Stoughton Children's Books
This edition first published 1986 by Knight Books (now Picture Knight)
Fourth impression 1989

Published by Hodder and Stoughton Paperbacks,
a division of Hodder and Stoughton Ltd,
Mill Road, Dunton Green, Sevenoaks, Kent TN13 2YA
Editorial office: 47 Bedford Square, London WC1B 3DP

Printed in Belgium by Proost International Book Production

This is a story about
Elfie—the best dog
in the whole world.

We grew up together, but Elfie grew
much faster than I did.

I loved resting my head on her warm
coat. Then we would dream together.

My brother and sister loved
Elfie very much, but she was
my dog.

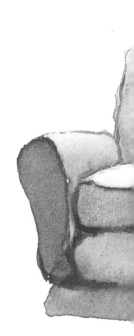

Every day, Elfie and I
played together.

Elfie loved to chase squirrels

and to dig in my mother's flower garden.

Sometimes my family would get very angry with Elfie when she got into mischief. But they still loved her, even when they scolded her.

The trouble was, they never told her. They thought Elfie knew that they loved her.

The years passed quickly, and while I was growing taller and taller, Elfie was growing rounder and rounder.

The older Elfie got,
the more she slept,
and the less
she liked to walk.
I was getting worried!

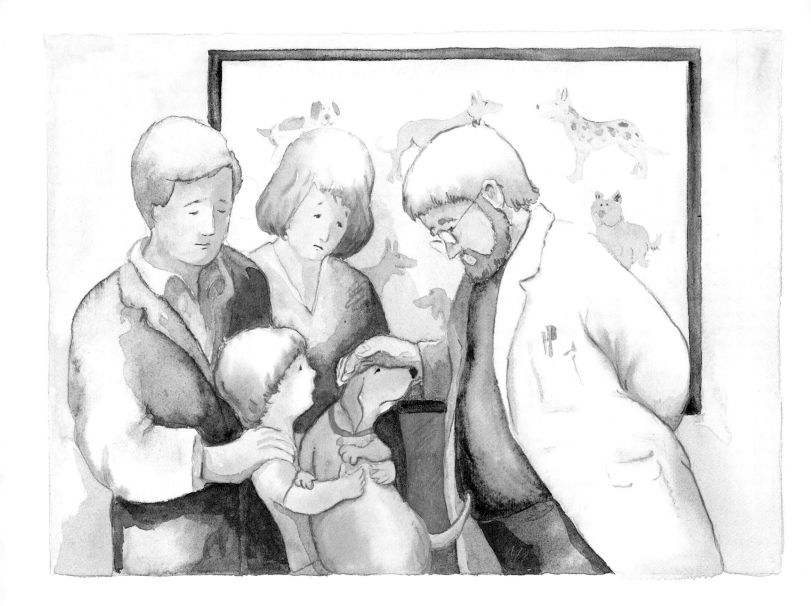

We took Elfie to the vet,
but there wasn't much he could do.
   "Elfie is just growing old,"
he said.

It soon became too difficult
for Elfie to climb the stairs.

But she *had* to sleep in my room.

I gave Elfie a soft pillow
to sleep on, and before
we went to sleep
I would say to her,
"I'll always love you."
I know she understood.

One morning I woke up
and discovered that Elfie
had died during the night.

We buried Elfie together.
We all cried and hugged
each other.

My brother and sister loved Elfie
a lot, but they never told her so.

I was very sad, too, but it helped
to remember that I had told her
every night, "I'll always love you."

A neighbour offered me a puppy.
I knew Elfie wouldn't
have minded, but I said no.

I gave him Elfie's basket instead.
He needed it more than I did.

Someday I'll have another dog,
or a kitten or a goldfish.
But whatever it is, I'll tell it
every night: "I'll always love you."

Some other Picture Knight books you may enjoy

Let's be Friends again!
Hans Wilhelm

My Dad doesn't even notice
Mike Dickinson

My Brother's Silly
Mike Dickinson

Smudge
Mike Dickinson

PRINTED IN BELGIUM BY
proost
INTERNATIONAL BOOK PRODUCTION